MW01205617

Before They Were President

BEFORE JOHN F. KENNEDY WAS PRESIDENT

Gareth Stevens
PUBLISHING

By Katie Kawa

Please visit our website, www.garethstevens.com. For a free color catalog of all our high-quality books, call toll free 1-800-542-2595 or fax 1-877-542-2596.

Library of Congress Cataloging-in-Publication Data

Names: Kawa, Katie, author.
Title: Before John F. Kennedy was president / Katie Kawa.
Description: New York : Gareth Stevens Publishing, 2018. | Series: Before they were president | Includes index.
Identifiers: LCCN 2017023000| ISBN 9781538210727 (pbk.) | ISBN 9781538210734 (6 pack) | ISBN 9781538210741 (library bound)
Subjects: LCSH: Kennedy, John F. (John Fitzgerald), 1917-1963–Juvenile literature. | Presidents–United States–Biography–Juvenile literature.
Classification: LCC E842.Z9 K39 2018 | DDC 973.922092 [B] –dc23
LC record available at https://lccn.loc.gov/2017023000

First Edition

Published in 2018 by
Gareth Stevens Publishing
111 East 14th Street, Suite 349
New York, NY 10003

Designer: Laura Bowen
Editor: Ryan Nagelhout/Kate Mikoley

Photo credits: Cover, p. 1 (John F. Kennedy) Alfred Eisenstaedt/The LIFE Picture Collection/Getty Images; cover, p. 1 (Kennedy compound) Tim Gray/Getty Images News/Getty Images; cover, pp. 1–21 (frame) Samran wonglakorn/ Shutterstock.com; p. 5 (main) Arnold Sachs/Archive Photos/Getty Images; pp. 5 (inset), 11 (inset) Hulton Archive/ Archive Photos/Getty Images; pp. 7, 13 Bettmann/Getty Images; p. 9 Basc catala/Wikimedia Commons; p. 11 (main) Jannis Tobias Werner/Shutterstock.com; p. 15 Hank Walker/The LIFE Picture Collection/Getty Images; p. 17 Scewing/ Wikimedia Commons; p. 19 (inset) GrahamHardy/Wikimedia Commons; p. 19 (main) Al Fenn/The LIFE Images Collection/ Getty Images; p. 21 (Kennedy) Spartan7W/Wikimedia Commons.

Printed in China

CPSIA compliance information: Batch #CW18GS: For further information contact Gareth Stevens, New York, New York at 1-800-542-2595.

CONTENTS

Words in the glossary appear in **bold** type the first time they are used in the text.

A YOUNG PRESIDENT

When people think of John F. Kennedy's life, they often think of how it ended. In 1960, he became the youngest man to be elected president of the United States. Three years later, he was killed in Dallas, Texas.

The rest of Kennedy's story, though, shouldn't be forgotten. His childhood, school years, and military service all played a part in his journey to the White House. Who was John F. Kennedy before he became president? Read on to find out!

People often called John F. Kennedy JFK.

JOHN F. KENNEDY AT AGE 10

John F. Kennedy was once a kid living in Massachusetts. He grew up to become one of the most famous US presidents.

A FAMOUS FAMILY

John Fitzgerald Kennedy was born on May 29, 1917, in Brookline, Massachusetts, which is near the city of Boston. He was the second of nine children born to Joseph and Rose Kennedy. John got his name from his grandfather on his mother's side, John Francis Fitzgerald, who once served as the mayor of Boston.

John was born into a very wealthy family. His father made millions of dollars as a businessman. He even worked in the movie business at one time!

John's great-grandparents came to the United States from Ireland.

Rose Kennedy grew up in the world of politics. She made sure her children learned about the history of American politics.

GROWING UP AS A KENNEDY

John, or Jack as he was sometimes called, was often sick as a child. That didn't keep him from having fun with his family when he could, though. The Kennedys spent a lot of time together. During the summer, they spent time at their home in Hyannis Port on the coast of Massachusetts.

Joseph Kennedy Sr. wanted his children to be the best at everything they did. He pushed them to **compete** with each other and to play hard.

Presidential Preview

When John was 2 years old, he got very sick with scarlet fever. This sickness was sometimes deadly, and John spent time in the hospital until he got better.

The Kennedys were an active family. They liked to sail, swim, and play sports such as football.

KENNEDY'S COLLEGE YEARS

John went to boarding school, or a school away from home, in Connecticut. In 1935, he started college at Princeton University. However, he soon became sick and had to leave school. The next year, he started studying at Harvard University. John played football at Harvard and liked studying history and government.

While John was at Harvard, his father was named US **ambassador** to England. John visited his father there and became even more interested in politics, history, and the military.

Presidential Preview

John wrote an important paper at Harvard about England at the start of World War II. That paper later became a book called *Why England Slept.*

JOHN AT COLLEGE

JOHN FOLLOWED IN HIS FATHER AND HIS OLDER BROTHER JOE'S FOOTSTEPS BY STUDYING AT HARVARD.

HARVARD CAMPUS

PT-109

John F. Kennedy **graduated** from Harvard in 1940. Then, he joined the US Navy. At that time, World War II was being fought around the world, and John was sent to the South Pacific. He was named commander of a boat known as *PT-109*.

In 1943, a Japanese boat hit *PT-109*, and it sank. Kennedy was hurt, but he still led his crew to safety. Because of his bravery, he was given the Navy and Marine Corps **Medal**.

Presidential Preview

In 1963, a movie was made about Kennedy's **heroism** during World War II. It was called *PT 109*.

John F. Kennedy became a war hero known for his strong leadership.

JFK IN NAVY UNIFORM

THE ROAD TO THE WHITE HOUSE

John wasn't the Kennedy who was supposed to become president. That dream belonged first to his older brother, Joe. However, Joe died while fighting in World War II. After his death, the family's hopes of having one of its own in the White House fell on John.

John began his **career** in politics by serving Massachusetts as a member of the US House of Representatives for 6 years, starting in 1947. Then, in 1953, he became a member of the US Senate.

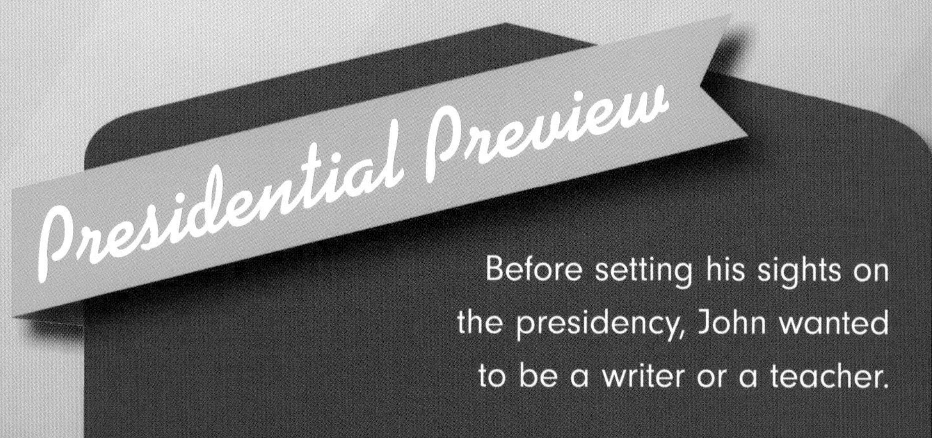

Before setting his sights on the presidency, John wanted to be a writer or a teacher.

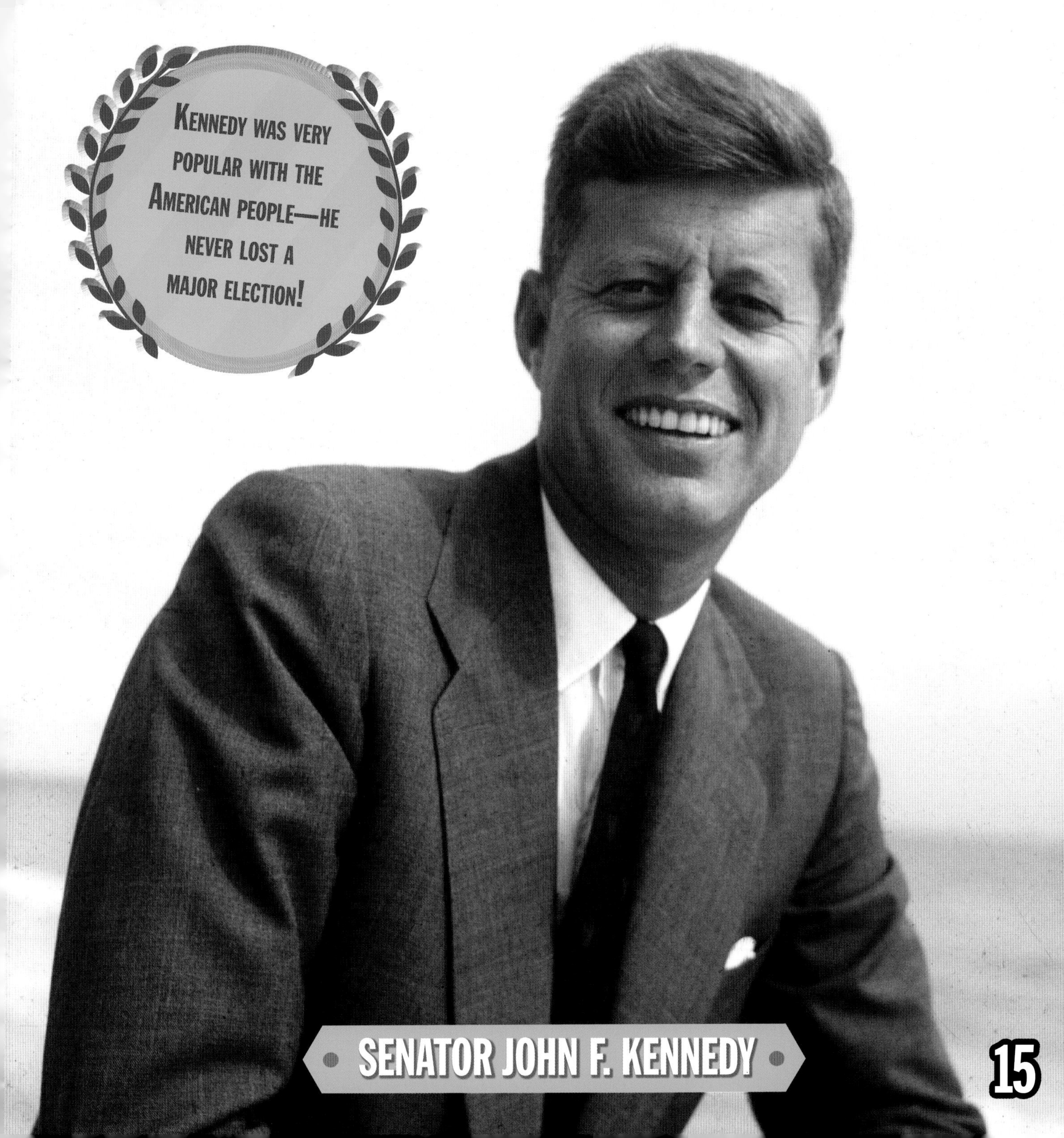

SENATOR JOHN F. KENNEDY

JACK AND JACKIE

The same year Kennedy began his career in the Senate, he married Jacqueline Bouvier. Jacqueline, often called Jackie, was a newspaper writer and **photographer** who also came from a wealthy family. They were married on September 12, 1953, in a church in Newport, Rhode Island.

In 1957, Jackie gave birth to the couple's first child, a daughter named Caroline. Three years later—just weeks after John was elected president—their son John F. Kennedy Jr. was born.

Presidential Preview

John and Jackie had a third child, Patrick, who was born in 1963. Sadly, he died when he was just 2 days old.

In the early 1960s, the Kennedys became the most famous young family in the United States. People enjoyed reading about and seeing pictures of John, Jackie, and their young children.

SUCCESS AS A WRITER

Not long after John and Jackie were married, he had **surgery** on his back. He hurt it for the first time when he was young and had problems with it for most of his life.

John had to spend time away from his work while healing. During this time, he wrote a book called *Profiles in Courage*. It was about US political leaders who fought for what they believed in. In 1957, his book won the Pulitzer Prize, a famous prize for writers.

Presidential Preview

Kennedy suffered from many sicknesses, had many surgeries, and dealt with pain for much of his life. However, he kept the truth about his health a secret because it might have harmed his political career.

Profiles IN Courage

Senator John F. Kennedy

WRITING *PROFILES IN COURAGE* ALLOWED KENNEDY TO LIVE OUT ONE OF HIS EARLY DREAMS OF BEING A WRITER WITHOUT GIVING UP HIS POLITICAL GOALS.

PRESIDENT KENNEDY

Kennedy knew the next step in his career was running for president. He set his sights on the 1960 election and worked very hard on the campaign trail.

Kennedy's hard work paid off, and he won the 1960 presidential election. He officially became the 35th president of the United States on January 20, 1961. His time in the White House was cut short when he was **assassinated**, but he is still known as one of America's most beloved leaders.

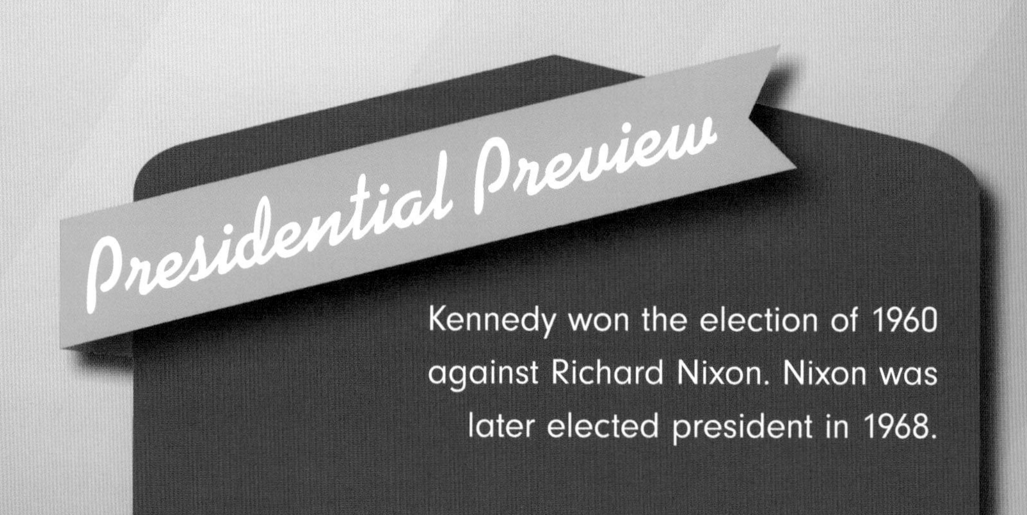

Presidential Preview

Kennedy won the election of 1960 against Richard Nixon. Nixon was later elected president in 1968.

Kennedy's Life: A Timeline

PRESIDENT KENNEDY

1917 John Fitzgerald Kennedy is born in Brookline, Massachusetts, on May 29.

1920 Kennedy becomes very sick with scarlet fever.

1935 Kennedy begins college at Princeton University, but has to leave because of health problems.

1936 Kennedy begins his time at Harvard University.

1940 Kennedy graduates from Harvard.

1943 Kennedy becomes a hero of World War II by helping save his fellow navy sailors on *PT-109* after the boat is sunk.

1947 Kennedy begins his career in the US House of Representatives.

1953 Kennedy becomes a US senator and marries Jacqueline Bouvier.

1957 Caroline Kennedy is born, and John's book, *Profiles in Courage*, wins the Pulitzer Prize.

1960 Kennedy is elected president, and John F. Kennedy Jr. is born.

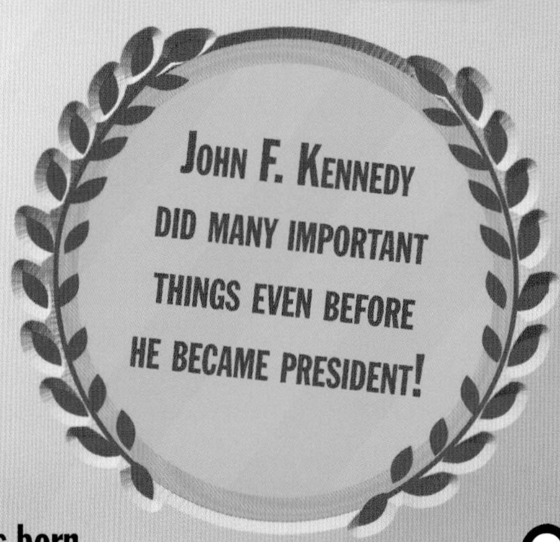

GLOSSARY

ambassador: a person sent to stand for their government's interests in another country

assassinate: to kill someone, especially a public figure

career: the job someone chooses to do for a long time

compete: to try to get or win something that another person is also trying to get or win

graduate: to finish a certain level of schooling, such as college

heroism: actions that are like those of a hero

medal: an honor or prize, often in the form of a flat, small piece of metal with art or words

photographer: a person who takes pictures with a camera

politics: the activities of the government and government officials

surgery: a medical operation that involves a doctor using tools to fix a problem inside the body

FOR MORE INFORMATION

Books

Duffield, Katy. *John F. Kennedy.* Mankato, MN: The Child's World, 2017.

Edison, Erin. *John F. Kennedy.* North Mankato, MN: Capstone Press, 2013.

Hansen, Grace. *John F. Kennedy.* Minneapolis, MN: Abdo Kids, 2015.

Websites

JFK's Early Years
content.time.com/time/photogallery/0,29307,1635575,00.html
This *TIME* magazine photo gallery features images from Kennedy's childhood through his wedding.

John F. Kennedy
www.whitehouse.gov/1600/presidents/johnfkennedy
The official White House webpage about John F. Kennedy features facts about his early life and presidency, and it also includes a link to learn more about Jackie Kennedy.

John F. Kennedy Presidential Library and Museum
www.jfklibrary.org
This website features facts and stories about Kennedy's life, as well as information to help you plan a trip to this library and museum in Massachusetts.

INDEX